THANKSGIVING COTTAGE

WRITTEN BY TERESA IVES LILLY

Follow Teresa and find out about FREE books at
www.teresalilly@wordpress.com

Meet the Branson Family
Mother Debra
Father Gerald

Oldest Son Ross

Next Oldest Son Greg
Greg's Wife Amy
Greg and Amy's Daughter; Shirley

Youngest Son Glen
Younger Sister Gwen

CHAPTER ONE

Jaimyn Jones sat at her desk in the office, listening to the other receptionists and secretaries all talking and laughing about their upcoming holiday plans. She kept her head down, so no one would notice she wasn't part of the conversation and ask about her plans.

Not because she wouldn't love to share plans with her friends and co-workers; for once feel as if she were part of the crowd, but that was the problem; She had no plans. Unlike those who were traveling to their homes for family gatherings, she, as always, would be spending her Thanksgiving alone.

Jaimyn looked up at the collage of photos over her desk, not one family member was represented there because she had no family members. Her mother had died when she was six and she'd basically raised herself since then, with little if no help from a few different foster and group home programs she'd been in and out of.

As far as she knew, there were no grandparents, aunts, uncles, cousins or other relatives on her mother's side and she never knew her father at all, so there had never been the excitement of 'going home' or to 'family gathering' for her. There were times as a child when she'd wished and prayed for the Thanksgiving holiday to have some meaning for her, but it never did.

A few times over the more recent years, she'd spent the Thanksgiving holidays with friends, but quickly felt as though she were a fifth wheel, out of place, not having been born into these families. So, now, she never let anyone know she had nowhere to go and no one to be with on Thanksgiving. She preferred being alone, to being the extra at the table.

Jaimyn had created her own tradition, usually spending the day cuddled in a chair, sipping cocoa and watching the Macy's parade and even the football game. Not because she liked football, but everyone in the office would be talking about it, and so she was able to converse about the one football game she watched each year and no one would know she hadn't been with family or friends for the holiday.

Jaimyn sat back with a sigh. Somehow, this year seemed harder than previous years she'd spent alone. The weather had been unusually warm in North West Texas and there was no chance of an early snow; which of course didn't come often in Western Texas. But, when the temperature was still in the 80s every day, it was hard to think about Thanksgiving.

"Jaimyn, just look at this picture." Her friend Kathy placed a magazine on the desk, opened to a photo of a mountain covered in snow with a lovely cabin tucked away under a big fir tree.

Jaimyn eyed it. "Looks cold." She pretended to shiver although she did think it was a beautiful scene. She'd never actually been any place like it in her life, so she had no idea how cold it could possibly be.

Kathy frowned. "I didn't mean that one." The woman flipped the book over to a page with a photo of a couple in bathing suits, swimming in a pool on a cruise liner.

"Hmm, that's a bit warmer." Jaimyn stated and gave her friend a big smile. Jaimyn had never been on a cruise either.

Kathy laughed. "Yep, well, that's what I'm doing this year. I talked Mom into booking enough rooms for the whole family on the cruise. We are spending Thanksgiving actually doing something I've always dreamed of." Kathy did a little happy dance then sat down on the chair beside Jaimyn.

Jaimyn closed her eyes, but a cruise was not the image that flashed through her mind. Instead, she saw a table; a long table with a brown table cloth over it and every inch completely covered with platters and plates of food. And around that table were friendly faces of people who knew her and loved her. That was the Thanksgiving she dreamed of.

The image slowly faded back to her own reality. "I'm glad you're getting your dream come true." She stated, trying to sound happy. Jaimyn had spent Thanksgiving with Kathy's family a few years ago and knew that they'd have a great time on the cruise. They weren't a typical old fashioned Thanksgiving type of family.

Kathy sat back and stared at Jaimyn.

Oh, no. Jaimyn thought*, she's just realized that I haven't told her what I'm doing for Thanksgiving.*

Kathy opened her mouth to ask the question, but Jaimyn pushed back her chair and stood up. "Think I'll go to the ladies' room." She whispered and slipped away quickly. The last thing she wanted was her best friend to feel sorry for her. In the past years, Jaimyn always made up some story about what she was going to do, but this year, she didn't feel like she could out and out lie about it.

Jaimyn looked up at the ceiling in the restroom. *You know Jesus, since becoming a believer, some things are more complicated. I know I shouldn't lie, but telling the truth in a case like this will only cause a big fuss. People in the office will feel bad and start offering to take me in for the holiday. But, that's not what I want, what I want is a holiday like the one I've always dreamed of.*

Jaimyn took her time in the ladies' room, hoping that when she got back to her desk, Kathy would have forgotten all about their conversation. Maybe she would have already headed home.

Finally, after ten minutes, she headed back to her desk. Kathy saw her across the room, but she was already hurrying out and gave a wave. Jaimyn smiled and waved back. When she sat back down, the magazine was still lying on her desk. Jaimyn turned it over and noted the picture of the cottage tucked away in the snow. Now, in her opinion, that would be the next best thing to having a family gathering, just getting away, to a cottage in the mountains, hidden by fir trees.

She lifted the magazine and gazed at it. Suddenly, her mind cried out, "And why not?"

It was almost the end of the day, and most of the others in the office had gone home. It was Monday, vacation for everyone began on Tuesday and ran until the following Tuesday. That was the nice part of working here, they gave great extended vacations. She wondered if there were any chance of her getting away, to a place like she'd seen in the magazine in time for Thanksgiving, but even if she couldn't go before Thanksgiving, maybe the day after.

Jaimyn clicked on her computer, typing in the words; Cottages for the Holiday. The computer instantly flashed and a whole long line of choices opened. However, from a quick glance, most of them were ads for places to stay for the Christmas Holidays. So, she retyped; Thanksgiving Cottages.

This time, there was only a few ads that appeared, however the first one seemed very interesting. When she clicked on the link, it opened to a very pleasant website, which boasted many unique Holiday Cottages on a one-hundred-acre evergreen farm located one mile outside of a town called Sprucewood, Colorado.

Each photo showed a cottage nestled among the spruce trees and each cottage was decorated specifically to match the name of the cottage. Some examples were: The Evergreen Cottage, The Gingerbread Cottage, The Sugar Cookie Cottage, The Candy Cane Cottage and others like that. Each one seemed to be a Christmas cottage theme by their names although they were available for rental all year long. The button at the bottom of each picture was not lit, instead the word RESERVED was written on the buttons, showing that each cottage was already taken. Her hopes began to drop, but what could she expect this close to the holidays.

She'd never been to Colorado but had always thought it would be pleasant to get away and see real snow on the mountains. Several friends had visited different places in Colorado and had shown her photos over the years like Denver, Durango, Crested Butte, Steamboat Springs and many other places. She'd always tucked the images away into her dreams for some day when she'd met someone and could go together. But that day had not come yet, so maybe it was time to go alone.

Finally, she clicked to the last page of the website and one of the newest cottages that had been added to the Holiday Cottages in the past few years, appeared. It was called the Thanksgiving Cottage.

Jaimyn's eyes lit up and she clicked on the photo of the cottage. The details came up on the screen.

The Thanksgiving Cottage is one of our newest cottages. A bit bigger than our standard cottages, this one is made just for you and your family to gather in to celebrate any holiday; especially Thanksgiving.

Beside the details were photos of the outside of the cottage and the inside, which consisted of four bedrooms, a large dining room, huge living room with a fireplace and a lovely kitchen, big enough for any family to be able to cook a full Thanksgiving meal in.

The rooms were all decorated in traditional Thanksgiving fashion, with patterns of turkeys, leaves and pumpkins. The bedrooms all had lovely fall themed quilts on the beds and according to the ad, each room was scented with pumpkin or holiday spice candle warmers.

Jaimyn sat back with a sign. This was her dream place, except that it was too big for just one person and she had no one to share it with. Of course, with the holidays starting the next day, she was pretty sure that the cottage wasn't even available.

She looked back at the computer screen. At the bottom, below the pictures, was the button, green with the word AVAILABLE written on it. She clicked on that and to her surprise, the cottage was not rented for this Thanksgiving.

It's crazy to even consider. Her thoughts whirled around in her head, but then again, she really didn't want to face her lonely apartment one more year for one more Thanksgiving. Just getting out of town would be worth the whole trip.

She clicked on the link that showed more about the area. There was a river called the Green Needle which ran from the town of Sprucewood, out and through the Evergreen Farm. There was also a scenic railroad train which ran along the outside edge of the farm all the way into town, called Little Valley Rails.

The town itself also had some pretty quaint names for its streets such as Spruce Street, Fir

Street, Evergreen Street and businesses such as; Dine in the Pines, Stitch in Time, Nature Pine Market, The Laundry Basket and the Silver Pine Tea Shoppe. All a bit quirky

Jaimyn sat back and took a breath. Her heart was actually beating with the excitement of the whole thing and that was something she hadn't felt for a long time. The idea of going to visit this town and stay in the Thanksgiving Cottage filled her soul. She tried to push the thoughts out of her mind, to convince herself it was impractical for her to go on a trip alone, but something continued to bring her eyes back to the pictures of the cottages.

I'd have to get a flight to the closest city. She clicked on the map. Sprucewood was about thirty miles from Golden Colorado which meant she could fly into Denver and rent a car and drive to the Evergreen Farm. That alone would be beautiful and peaceful.

Again, her hand hovered over the mouse. Was this just too crazy? Jaimyn knew she needed a break from her typical boring Thanksgiving and even if all she did was cuddle up by a fireplace in the Thanksgiving cottage, it would be different. Maybe there would be a quaint church hosting a Thanksgiving dinner she could attend. It would be nice, to share the day with other Christians which was something her pastor had recommended in service this past weekend. She had considered signing up to join a few others from her church, but at the last minute she didn't do it since she was so new to the church.

Pulling up another tab on the computer and searching for flights to Denver, she was shocked to find there were still seats available. It was obvious there was nothing to stop her from going on this trip, not even money. She'd been saving for years, not for anything special, but she didn't usually go on trips so spending a bit on this holiday wasn't going to hurt her.

Before leaving the office, Jaimyn had rented the Thanksgiving Cottage; although she'd had a few problems with the website. Once or twice the button on the screen had flicked from AVAILABLE to RESERVED, but she was finally able to get it to go through and give her a reservation confirmation. Then she bought a straight flight ticket to fly into Denver and had a rental car ready.

That night as she lay in bed, she suddenly slipped off the side of three bed onto her knees. She didn't pray that way often, but there were times when she felt such a closeness to her Savior that she wanted to reverence Him this way. This was one of those nights. She was so thankful that everything about the Thanksgiving Cottage and flights had worked out.

Lord, thank you for allowing me to find this Thanksgiving Cottage for the holiday. Please help me to use that time to grow closer to You.

Finally, she crawled into bed and fell asleep with images of that lovely Thanksgiving cottage filling her mind

CHAPTER TWO

The plane's takeoff was smooth and Jaimyn was finally able to unbuckle her seatbelt and relax. The man in the seat next to her had instantly fallen asleep, so she didn't expect to have to chit chat on the flight.

Just then, a small hand slipped onto hers. Jaimyn looked down, in the main aisle, standing beside her seat was a cute little girl, about five years old, smiling up at her.

"Hi." The child said.

Jaimyn smiled back. "Hi yourself."

The girl moved a step closer. "We's goin to Denber."

"Really, I'm going to Denver too."

"We's gonna have turkwey. Are you?"

Jaimyn nodded. "I hope so."

"Shirley, go back to your seat." A stern voice interrupted the conversation between Jaimyn and the child.

"Ok, Uncle Ross." The child stuck her thumb in her mouth, turned and disappeared into a row of seats three behind Jaimyn.

"I'm sorry if she was bothering you." The man's voice was deep and a bit harsh.

Jaimyn lifted her eyes and met his. "She was no

bother." Her voice trailed off as her mind took in the handsome face. He was tall and had a clean short almost black crew cut with a beautiful face. She found him almost irresistible, from his chin to his blue icy eyes. "I suppose it's a bit boring on an airplane for a child." Jaimyn stated.

"Hmm. Yes, but she does know better." The man turned on his heels and walked away.

Too bad, he's such a grump. He's very easy on the eyes. Jaimyn shook her head. That was a silly thought. It didn't matter what the man looked like. He was a total stranger and she'd probably never see him again. She could only hope he wasn't mean to the child. She seemed a sweet imp.

Before landing, Jaimyn headed to the lavatory. On her way, she saw the little girl snuggled in a seat between another girl about thirteen and a boy about sixteen. The young girl's eyes lit up.

"That's the lady I talked to." She announced. The two teens turned and looked at Jaimyn. They both smiled.

The handsome man who had been so abrupt was in the seat behind them, sitting beside a lovely blond woman. *Just the type of woman a man like him would have as a wife.* Jaimyn mused. There was an empty seat beside her on the other side.

Jaimyn was so busy thinking about the man and his wife, she didn't pay attention to where she was going and suddenly, bumped into someone.

She looked up and met the eyes of another man. This man was a bit shorter than the other. He had light brown hair and brown eyes. He was handsome as well.

"Excuse me, Miss." The man squeezed by her.

Well, I never thought of looking for handsome men on an airplane before. She almost started giggling at her own thoughts as she turned to let the man by. Jaimyn watched as he moved down the aisle, then squeezed in to sit in the empty seat beside the blonde woman. Now she wondered, which one was the woman's husband.

Again, shaking these thoughts away, she entered the lavatory at the same moment the lights on the plane flashed for everyone to have their seatbelts on. She hurried and rushed back up the aisle, but an older gentleman reached out and stopped her. "Miss, I've been told that our granddaughter was bothering you." Jaimyn could hardly believe it. This man, although in his sixties, was ruggedly handsome as well.

"She did not bother me. She's precious." Jaimyn could see the resemblance between the mad with the icy blue eyes and this one, who was obviously the other's father.

The man's wife leaned forward. "Thank you. We love her. This is her first time to fly. We weren't sure how she would do and we didn't want her to be a problem."

"I think she did great." Jaimyn answered and then walked back to her seat. The man beside her had still not begun to stir and her sitting down didn't awaken him. She buckled her seatbelt to prepare for landing, closed her eyes and pictured each of the members of the family in the seats behind her.

That is one nice family. She thought. *Probably flying to Denver for a big family gathering.*

A frown flit across her face. Once more the idea of a big family Thanksgiving filled her mind, although she knew it was not to be a reality for her this year or any time soon, but in her thoughts, she now had faces she could place around the table of her imaginings.

However, she wasn't too sure that the first man, with the icy blue eyes, would be included. Something about him disturbed her; well at least, something about him made her heart seem to tighten and she felt a bit breathless around him. Whether that was a good thing or not, she didn't expect to ever find out.

~

The Denver airport was crowded as well and, in a way, it was amusing to see how different people were dressed. Those heading out to warmer weather states like Florida wore short sleeved shirts and light jackets, while those flying into Denver had on heavy winter sweaters and over coats.

Jaimyn had looked at the weather ahead of time and finding there was a chance of light snow, she dressed accordingly. She didn't plan to be out roaming around in snow drifts, but she made sure to pack a warm coat and boots in case of an emergency.

As she stood in line to get her rental car, she decided that the turtle neck and jeans had been a good choice. She'd even passed on wearing heels and had slipped on a pair of cowboy boots she kept for the very rare occasion that she and a friend would go out dancing.

As she waited, she noted the family from the airplane gathering nearby. They were probably getting a car as well. For a moment, she wondered where they would be spending the holidays, but her thoughts were cut short when the man at the counter looked up with a grim smile. "Can I help you?"

"I'm here to get a car? My name is Jaimyn Jones."

The man clicked a few buttons on his computer. "Jeep?" He glanced up at her.

She shrugged. Not sure what kind of vehicle she

would need.

"Where you going?"

"Sprucewood Colorado."

The man stopped typing. "Really? That's a great little town. Wow, I wish I were going there for the holidays it's really nice."

Jaimyn smiled. "It's my first time, but I'm hoping to enjoy it."

"You will and yes, I think a jeep is your best bet."

In minutes Jaimyn was in the jeep and heading out of Denver west toward Golden. There were a few snowflakes falling, which made her smile. It only snowed at home once in a while and never really built up. She could see that these flurries were sticking to the ground and not melting right away.

It took forty minutes to get to Golden, where she stopped for a few minutes to rest. She drove up the main street and stopped at a restaurant for a bite to eat. From the window of the restaurant, she could see the mountains nearby. They were beautiful. Sprucewood was another twenty-minute drive, further up in the mountains and then another ten minutes to the cottages. Luckily, she'd arrive before dark.

Suddenly, it occurred to her that she had nothing to cook for Thanksgiving. In past years, she'd usually purchased a Turkey Dinner at Bill Miller's Barbeque restaurant and had it on hand for the day, but here she wasn't sure what she would do.

Well, I hope I can find something in Sprucewood. She thought as she drove toward the cottages.

~

Sprucewood was a quaint place. As Jaimyn drove through the streets, she noted that the houses had front porches with rocking chairs and wide front lawns with friendly looking sidewalks. Many yards were decorated with scarecrows left over from Halloween. As she reached the center of the city, were the streets formed a square around City Hall; a large red brick building, she had to smile. It gave her a feeling of home as most of the older towns in Texas were built around a City Hall the same way.

It was nice to see the actual stores that went along with the names she'd only read on the website. On Pine Street there was a café called Dine in the Pines. Perhaps she would be able to order a Thanksgiving meal from there. Beside that was a quilt store called Stitch in Time, alongside a very small grocery store called Nature Pine Market and a laundry mat called The Laundry Basket.

It almost didn't seem real to her that such a place could even exist.

When she reached the Holiday Cottage's Farm

she turned into the driveway. The first building was a small shop with a sign that simply read, "Gifts." She had a map she'd printed off the internet and was able to follow a small road that led to the right. She passed several other cottages, which were small intimate cottages, but when she reached the end of the road, there was the Thanksgiving Cottage. It was much bigger than the previous cottages, yet it wasn't ostentatious.

Jaimyn pulled the jeep up into one of the parking spots, turned off the engine and sat back, just staring at the cottage. It was lovely. The large cottage had a front porch which was decorated with pumpkins and fall colored garland.

She'd been sent a text telling her the keys would be in the door, so Jaimyn slid out of the car and traipsed to the cottage. She turned the key and opened the door then stepped into a large open living room with a huge fireplace on the opposite wall. There was a small, jovial fire burning and from the aroma of pumpkin spice, she assumed there was a wax warmer somewhere plugged in.

To the left was the kitchen and across the hallway to the left was the dining room. Jaimyn stopped in front of it, her mouth dropped open. This was the room she'd always seen in her dreams whenever she'd pictured a big family dinner. Even to the exact dishes she'd imagined.

She moved back into the living room and flopped onto the overstuffed comfy chair and sat staring at the fire. She was finally here, in her dream holiday cottage, but once again, she was alone.

She bent her head. *Lord, will I always be alone?*

Jaimyn closed her eyes. It had been a long day, she just wanted to cuddle up in the chair and take a little nap.

~

Not sure what it was, but something woke her. Jaimyn sat up, at first confused, not sure where she was. The noise seemed to be coming from behind her. She stood up and turned around, realizing just where she was and at the same time, that she was no longer alone.

Standing inside the doorway of the cottage, were eight familiar faces.

Jaimyn blinked, unable to make sense of what she was seeing.

Finally, a small child trotted forward and took her hand. "We's come to have Thanksgiving here. Are you having Thanksgiving here too?"

Jaimyn lifted her eyes from the child and scanned the people in front of her. Every one of them had a welcoming, warm smile on their face, except one.

The man stepped forward, his icy blue eyes almost freezing her with his stare.

"May I ask, what you are doing in our Thanksgiving Cottage."

CHAPTER THREE

Jaimyn's mouth dropped open as she gazed at the family standing in the front room of the cottage. Finally, she was able to squeak out, "Your cottage? I booked this cottage for the holiday."

The man crossed his arms over his chest. "I don't see how that could be. I booked it just the other night."

"So did I." She stood a little straighter, insulted by his tone. "What time did you book it?"

"About five, from my office."

"So, did I. There was a glitch that night. For a moment it showed booked. But then came back to available. It looks like we both booked at the same time, and the computer didn't know what to do."

The man stepped forward. "Well, as you can see, I have an entire family here with me. I can't very well book someplace big enough for us all at this short notice. You could probably find something else."

Now Jaimyn was getting pretty upset. She jammed her hands onto her hips. "Look. I'm not going anywhere. This is my dream cabin for the holidays. I don't want to be rude, but I'm not going to be kicked out like a feral cat."

Just then, the other gentleman Jaimyn had seen

on the plane stepped forward. "Excuse me, Miss?"

"Jaimyn. You can call me Jaimyn."

The man cleared his throat. "Jaimyn. I'm sorry this has happened, but before we get into a fist fight, why don't we all sit down and talk this out?"

She nodded, and the whole troupe moved further into the cabin. What had seemed too big earlier, suddenly started to feel much smaller. Little Shirley ran across the room and hugged Jaimyn. "I think you's pwetty. I like you."

Jaimyn smiled at the child. "I like you too."

"Good, we can all have Thanksgwiving togefer." She turned and ran over to the man she'd called Uncle Ross, earlier. "Uncle Ross, I like her. It will be fun to have Thansgwiving wiff her."

The child's upturned face was precious and Jaimyn wondered if anyone ever refused her anything. Anyone except Uncle Ross. His stern demeanor didn't seem to be moved by her desire.

The family all sat on chairs or the sofa around the room. The other man spoke again. "By the way, my name is Greg Branson. This is my family. My parents; Debra and Gerald. My younger brother Glen and sister Gwen and this is my wife Amy and you've already met my daughter Shirley."

Jaimyn smiled at each person and for some reason seemed overly pleased to know that the lovely blonde was Glen's wife and not Uncle

Ross' wife. "My name is Jaimyn." She stated loud enough for them all to hear.

Greg nodded in acknowledgement then went on. "And this is my older brother, by only one year; Ross."

Jaimyn couldn't help but wonder why Ross wasn't named something that started with a G. The look of confusion must have seemed familiar because Glen laughed slightly. "Ross chooses to use his middle name. His real name is Gabriel."

Her mouth formed an o. That must have been a hard name to have had as a child. She could imagine other kids mocking him for being named after God's angel Gabriel. However, she knew that his name meant *A Hero of God.*

Just then Ross interjected. "Okay Glen, we are introduced. Now, what are we going to do about her being here?"

Jaimyn felt like she'd been slapped across the face. The man may be handsome, and had a great name, but he was just rude.

Greg ran a hand through his hair. "What Ross said about finding another place for our family is true. We searched high and low for this one. I don't think we or you could find anything before Thanksgiving. I for one vote that we all spend it together. Would that be acceptable to you?"

Jaimyn scanned the faces of the others. Most of

them were smiling at her, or nodding their heads in agreement. A flash of family around the large table went through her mind. This could very well be the only chance she would ever have to fulfill that dream, although she didn't want to be the outsider.

Jaimyn looked up at Greg. "I think it would be alright. However, I insist on being treated as part of the family. I want to help prepare the meal, and anything else that is a holiday tradition in your family."

Greg's wife stood up and walked over to her and took her hand. "Jaimyn, you have no idea what you just asked for. Remember, I've been in your position before and you can't even imagine all the tradition that goes into a Branson Family Thanksgiving. But, I for one, will be happy to have another pair of willing hands to help."

Greg looked around the room. "Everyone in favor of Jaimyn sharing Thanksgiving with us, raise your hand."

Jaimyn watched as all their hands shot into the air at once, except Ross' hand. She glared at him.

"Well, I've been out voted, so I guess we will all share Thanksgiving together." He turned and stomped away.

Jaimyn clenched her hands. She just wanted to yell at his back, but she realized there was no use. She turned back to the family with a weak smile.

"So, this will all be very new to me. I have not family so I don't know what a family does, for Thanksgiving or any other time."

Debra, the mother of the group moved across the room and pulled Jaimyn into her arms and gave her a hug and whispered in her ear. "We are going to have a wonderful time and you are already a special gift from God to us."

Jaimyn stepped back and met the woman's eyes. "You are a believer?" She asked in a hushed tone.

"A Jesus loving believer."

Jaimyn could feel the spirit in her begin to rejoice. "I'm a new believer."

The woman hugged her again. "Well then, Jaimyn. Welcome to the family; God's family and the Branson family.

She felt as if she could stay in this mother's embrace forever. She'd longed for a mother's love for so long. Her eyes filled with tears, but she blinked them back. Crying wasn't going to be the way she wanted to start her relationship with this family.

Greg spoke up again. "Then, if this is all settled, shall we carry our bags up to the rooms. Of course, we may have to make a change to our original room assignments."

Jaimyn moved closer to him. "I don't have to stay in the master bedroom. I'm content anywhere." She looked around. It would be awkward to share a room with married couples.

"The younger girl Gwen spoke up. "Why not share my room. Shirley will sleep with me in the full bed on the bottom bunk. You can sleep on the top?"

"That sounds great. I've always wanted a younger sister."

Debra looked at her seriously. "Are you sure? We can squeeze a few more together so you can have a room to yourself?"

"Nope, I like this idea. Really. It will make me feel like I'm part of the family." Jaimyn gave the woman a hug this time, then turned back to Gwen. "Come on, let's go get my bags out of the master room and get ourselves settled."

The other girl nodded.

"What about me?" Shirley jealously stomped her foot.

"You too, imp." Jaimyn laughed and patted the girl's head.

"Uncle Ross calls me imp, too." She giggled and took Jaimyn's hand. They all three headed toward the stairs and made their way up to the master bedroom. When they reached the master bed room, Jaimyn noticed Ross standing by the door. His lips formed a grim line.

"I expected my parents to sleep here. This whole

holiday was set up especially for them. We always have a get together, but never have done one away from home. This was supposed to be so special." His words tore at her soul.

"I just came up to move my belongings. I'm joining the girls in their room." She pictured him choking on his words.

His head lifted up and they met eye to eye. "Oh, well, thank you. That will mean a lot to them." He began to move toward the stairs. "Sorry I must seem like a real ogre to you. I just wanted this holiday to be perfect, for mom."

"I understand; and if it appears that I'm not fitting enough, I'll find another place. I'm looking forward to being part of the family though." Her voice almost had a pleading tone to it. She wanted the man to understand her desire for a family Thanksgiving.

"I appreciate that. I think it should be alright. Mom seems to like you and so…" he didn't say anymore, just turned away and began to go down the stairs.

Jaimyn just stared at his back, then shook her head. The man was an enigma to her. He seemed so harsh, and yet he was obviously concerned for his mother's sake that this be a wonderful family holiday.

Lord, I don't know if this is answer to my

prayers for having a real family Thanksgiving, but I thank You for the opportunity. Help me and Ross to find a common ground so that we can both enjoy this holiday.

With that, Jaimyn picked up the suitcase she'd set down and hurried to the room down the hall. She'd never slept in a bunkbed before. She imagined its size was going to be a bit tight for her, but she was going to consider it a highlight of a new adventure.

"Look, Jaimyn. You's gonna sweep up there." Shirley pointed at the top bunk. "It's too high for me." The girl plopped her thumb into her mouth and gave a little suck.

"I think it's going to be wonderful. I'm glad there's a ladder." She placed her suitcase on the floor and decided to try to get up onto the bunk before making a definite decision. The ladder was pretty sturdy and she was able to crawl up and lay down. The mattress was surprisingly comfortable.

"What do you think?" Gwen asked.

"Hmm, I think I could fall asleep right now. It's comfy up here. I don't toss and turn too much so I shouldn't keep you awake."

"Well, I'm sleeping with Shirley and she does toss and turn, so I'll be fighting her feet all night." Gwen and Jaimyn both laughed. Shirley didn't understand the conversation but she burst out with a fake laugh as well.

The girls spend a few more minutes getting their clothes out of the suitcases and splitting the closet and the bureau. Everything fit just fine, and they tucked their empty suitcases in the back of the closet.

"Now, that's done, let's go see if we can help in the kitchen. Dads probably already brought in the groceries we picked up on the way here. Tonight, we have mom's famous Branson lasagna and tomorrow we start preparing for Thanksgiving." Gwen stepped out of the room, Shirley skipped behind her and Jaimyn followed them. Part of her felt very young, as if she were actually a sister to these girls.

Shirley turned back to Jaimyn. "This year I's big 'nough to help. I'm going to stuff the twurkey."

Jaimyn laughed. "That sounds like fun." She turned to Gwen again. "I've never made a Thanksgiving meal; what do you think we'll have to do?" She asked.

Gwen smiled. "Everything. We have to make pies, get the turkey defrosted and prepare stuffing. Peel potatoes and have them ready to mash, get the green bean casserole made and into the refrigerator."

"That is a lot. I've never done any of it before, so you'll have to be patient with me and help me figure it all out."

"Sure, just having you here will take some of the work off my shoulders. The men don't do any of the cooking. They mostly watch sports and run errands. However, we stocked up really well at the store on our way in because Ross says it might snow and we don't want to risk not being able to get back to the store."

Jaimyn's eyes grew large. She hadn't thought of that at all. It made her a bit nervous imagining herself snowed in here, without any food since she hadn't gone and gotten any yet.

"I'm glad you all thought of everything." She sounded thankful.

"And just wait 'til you taste Gwandma's pumpkin pie. It's the best." Shirley sang out as she disappeared into the kitchen.

Jaimyn could hardly wait.

CHAPTER FOUR

Jaimyn; unused to so many people, felt as if everywhere she moved, she was bumping

into someone, so she stepped back into a corner and just watched.

The bags of groceries were on the counter and Debra and Gwen were busy unpacking them. Cold items were put into the refrigerator, while canned items were stacked on the counter.

From what she could see, there were yams, green beans, fried onions, cream of mushroom soup, canned gravy, potatoes, milk, butter, rolls, turkey, stuffing, canned pumpkin, pecans, pie shells, whipped cream, and so much more.

"This is going to be some glorious meal." Jaimyn couldn't refrain from saying.

Debra laughed. "Once we get busy cooking it all, you may not think it's so great. We cook for hours and it only take about thirty minutes for everyone to eat their fill. It's not very satisfying in that sense.

"I've never had a chance to make any of those things. I usually order myself a small turkey dinner from Bill Millers. So, for me, this is a great opportunity."

Gwen turned around. "Mom, I have no problem allowing Jaimyn to take over for me. I wouldn't mind a year off."

"I think we can each share our load with Jaimyn but I don't think you need to give up all the fun." She laughed.

Gwen shrugged. "Can't blame me for trying to get out of work. I mean, the guys don't do anything."

"That is the lot in life for women at Thanksgiving. Remember, your father does carve the turkey."

Just then Amy came into the kitchen. "Shirley, Daddy is going to take the men out for a walk to look over the farm, do you want to go with them?"

The child nodded. "Yes." She turned to look at her grandmother. "You's not gonna stuff the twurkey today?"

Debra bent over and kissed the child's forehead. "Nope. I'm going to make the lasagna now. Tomorrow morning, we will work on the food and Thursday we will stuff the turkey."

"Okay." Shirley seemed content and skipped away holding her mother's hand.

Debra faced Jaimyn and Gwen. "You girls can go outside with the men if you want."

Gwen shook her head. "No, this year I want to learn how to make your lasagna. Last year I didn't pay attention and I want to add it to my future recipe box." She looked at Jaimyn. "How about you?"

"I'd rather stay here and learn how to cook lasagna as well, if you don't mind." She didn't want to mention that she wasn't up to facing Ross and his anger again.

Debra smiled. "That's great. We can get this done quickly and be ready for the evening board games."

Jaimyn tilted her head. "Board games?"

"Yes, we brought about ten of them. Whenever we are all together, we break into groups and play board games."

Jaimyn felt anticipation flood her. That was something she'd always wanted to do but never had a chance.

"Of course, don't play Monopoly with Ross, you'll never win." Gwen laughed.

Debra shook her head. "We don't bring Monopoly anymore." She glared at Gwen. "You are going to frighten Jaimyn. Ross isn't that bad."

"Mom, seriously? When it comes to Monopoly, my brother has no mercy. Even when I was five years old, he would beat me. Most older brothers will let a girl win once in a while, but not Ross, he's a cutthroat."

Jaimyn watched as Debra's lips began to twitch. "Okay, I admit it. Ross does get a bit competitive when it comes to that game. However, he is rather well behaved with the other games."

For the next hour, Jaimyn watched and assisted as Debra demonstrated the intricacies of lasagna making. She would never have guessed it was so detailed. After just a few minutes, she asked for a blank paper so she too could write out the recipe for future use.

Someday, maybe I'll be married and can serve this.

~

After helping to prepare the meal, Jaimyn headed upstairs. She wanted to freshen up before dinner was served. It had been an eye-opening experience watching a true talented cook create something.

Shirley had been napping earlier but she'd waken before Jaimyn entered the room. The little girl bounced up and down on the bed. "Jaimwnn, I took a nap."

"That's good. Are you ready for dinner?"

The girl nodded. "I don't like Zonya."

Jaimyn sat on the bed beside her. "Really, I got to taste it and it was really good."

The child stared at her. "You sure?"

Jaimyn swished her hand across her chest. "Cross my heart. I tell you what. How about you try one big bite?"

"Okay. But if I don't like it, Gwandma makes me chicken nuggets."

"Mmm, that sounds good too."

The bedroom door was open and Ross walked by. "Jaimyn, do you need some privacy? I can take Shirley down with me?"

Jaimyn shook her head. "No, I don't mind her being here, but if she'd ready to go down, and you are going down…"

Shirley slipped off the bed. "I'm weady, Uncle Ross. Guess what?"

The man couldn't help but smile. "What?"

"I'm gonna twy Zonya."

The man looked impressed and lifted his head to meet Jaimyn's eyes. "Is this your doing?"

She nodded.

"Well, you must be a miracle worker." He actually stepped into the room and stared at her. She felt her cheeks blush.

Ross held out his hand and Shirley slipped hers into his. They turned and left the room, but before they got completely out, Ross looked over his shoulder and silently mouthed, "Thank you."

When they were out of site, Jaimyn lifted her hand to her cheek to see if it was burning, but it was cool.

Why do I feel so strange around that man? He's infuriating, but then when he's nice, I get all flustered and embarrassed.

"Where shall I sit?" Jaimyn asked as she entered the kitchen again and nodded toward the dining room table.

"Shirley has already claimed your company." Amy stated as she helped carry the large pan of lasagna to the dining room.

Jaimyn grabbed the big bowl of salad and followed Amy. Everyone was already seated, so Jaimyn slid into the chair beside Shirley. The little girl was sitting on a stack of books to lift her up higher.

"Look Jaimwn. I'm bigger now."

Jaimyn laughed.

Once they were all seated, Debra suggested Gerald lead them in prayer. Jaimyn looked around to see their faces. She wondered if all of them were Christians or only Debra. No one blinked at the request, but that didn't tell her what she wanted to know.

Gerald led them in a very short prayer and then began serving himself from the lasagna pan. The entire meal was wonderful and the family's chatter was entertaining. Jaimyn didn't have to talk much, but she learned plenty about the different members of the family, all except Ross. It seemed that the family knew he didn't like to have his past talked about.

There was one moment though when Shirley asked Ross if he had a gwirlfriend. All eyes at the table turned on him. Ross didn't speak at first, then finally laughed and said, "Yes, Shirley. You are my girlfriend."

Everyone released their breath and the talk went on, but Shirley turned to Jaimyn with a huge smile. "Uncle Ross needs a gwirlfriend. Can't you be his gwirlfriend?"

Jaimyn leaned in closer. "Shhh. I don't think Uncle Ross would like to hear you saying that."

Shirley's lower lip pouted out. "Well, I want you to be his gwirlfriend." She crossed her arms over her chest. Jaimyn had to hold her breath to keep from laughing out loud. She was glad that the meal was over and that games would start soon.

Shirley was herded off to bed for the evening which made Jaimyn glad. She was afraid the child would say something silly about her being Ross' girlfriend in front of him.

Glen and Gwen got out the boardgames. It was decided that they would play Scattergories.

Many times, during the game, Glen or Greg or Ross made up silly words that didn't actually work for the game, but made everyone laugh. It was interesting to see the other side of Ross. The men in this family were surely fun.

When the game was over and everyone had headed to bed, Jaimyn lay in the top bunk bed trying to relive the entire day, since the moment she met Shirley on the airplane. It had been a wonderful day meeting and getting to know the Branson family.

Debra had indicated that the next day would be even better as they prepared food for the next day's Thanksgiving meal. Shirley told her that she planned to find the wishbone and that she and Jaimyn could make a Thanksgiving wish.

That seemed like a fun tradition and she did hope to be able to share it with Shirley. A part of Jaimyn's heart ached because she knew this wonderful family time would end once the holiday was over and she'd go back home, to continue living alone and future holidays would be spent alone.

Even if she booked cottages every holiday, there would never be another one like this one spent with the Branson family. A single tear rolled down her cheek but she angrily brushed it away. There was no point in crying over the life God had given her. Until today, she didn't even think she was missing anything.

Jaimyn rolled over on her stomach and forced herself to stop thinking, but as she drifted off, the sound of Ross's earlier laughter filled her thoughts.

CHAPTER FIVE

The next morning, Greg, Gerald, Glen and Ross cooked breakfast for the ladies. There were scrambled eggs, bacon, biscuits and fresh fruit. Jaimyn was very impressed.

"What's wrong, don't you think men can cook?" Ross looked down his nose at her and asked.

"Sure, I mean, I've never experienced it before, but I'm not an expert."

"On men cooking or on men in general?"

Jaimyn's dropped open at the question.

"Ross, that wasn't very nice." His mother stated.

Ross shook his head. "I didn't mean it the way it sounded."

"It doesn't matter." Jaimyn answered. "And to answer, both."

Once again, the frown formed on Ross' forehead and Jaimyn was left feeling as if she had said something wrong.

"Girls, the men had their turn in the kitchen, now it's our chance. That Thanksgiving meal won't get prepared without us." Debra announced and the girls all stood up and began to clear the table.

As she passed him, Jaimyn stopped beside Ross. "Thanks for breakfast." She said and headed into the kitchen.

~

Debra plopped a recipe book on the counter. "One thing at a time. The pies need to be made and the turkey prepped. Amy, you make a great green bean casserole, so you work on that." Then she turned to Gwen and Jaimyn. "Why don't you girls work on peeling the potatoes?"

Gwen handed a peeler to Jaimyn, but Jaimyn just stared at it.

"Do you know how to peel a potato?" Gwen asked.

"Yes, with a knife, but I've never used a peeler."

Gwen gave her a quick lesson and the girls began to work happily. Jaimyn was pleased at her progress with the peeler.

Twenty minutes later, Ross entered the kitchen. Jaimyn looked up; her own smile faded. He seemed to be staring at her and his look was one of anger.

"Mother. This is supposed to be your vacation. You girls can handle all the cooking, can't you?" His voice boomed out, but Jaimyn felt his eyes were on her and that his words were directed at her specifically.

"Ross, I'm fine. I love cooking the Thanksgiving meal." Debra assured him.

Ross touched his mother's shoulder. "But I don't want you getting overly tired."

Debra moved across the room and took his hand. "Ross, I'm fine, really. I promise if I get tired, I will sit down to rest. Having another set of hands in the kitchen is making everything easier. Why last year, I had to peel all the potatoes myself."

Jaimyn felt a warmth of pleasure spread through her heart at the woman's words. She couldn't understand why Ross was being so pushy, however, she turned and watched Debra for a few minutes. The woman's face was pale. Maybe she was sick."

"I don't mind doing more if someone just tells me what to do." Jaimyn's words were meant for Ross and he knew it. The scornful look disappeared and was replaced by a humbled look.

"Thank you, again." He gave his mother a quick hug, turned and left the room.

"What a grump Uncle Ross is being." Gwen stated. She turned and surveyed her mother. "Are you sure you feel up to this, Mom?"

Debra nodded. "All I'm doing is mixing up the ingredients for pies."

Gwen watched her for a few minutes, then turned back to the job at hand. "Mom was pretty sick for a month. She had some kind of virus and she ended up in the hospital for two weeks. It's only been a few weeks since. We came here so that she didn't have to work so hard to get the house all ready for the holiday. This place was already decorated and had clean sheets, so Ross jumped at it."

Jaimyn tilted her head in understanding. "I'm glad she's feeling better, but it's good to know. Now, we will just make a pact to do all we can to help her."

Gwen reached over and gave Jaimyn a hug. "I agree with Shirley. I like you. The whole family likes you."

Jaimyn's heart beat happily, but she did wonder if the whole family included Ross. His icy blue eyes told her a different story. He didn't like her being here.

~

As preparations went on and on, Glen, Greg, Gerald and even Ross came and went. Tasting things, they could, grabbing bags of chips and sodas. There were family jokes tossed out in passing and many stories told about past holidays. Jaimyn was tired, but having the time of her life. This was the first time she didn't feel like a fifth wheel at a holiday event, and even though she wasn't a real family member, they all made her feel so welcome; she was able to convince herself that she was really wanted.

The only one who was reserved around her was

Ross. It seemed that all he could do was glare at her and say uncomfortable things, which he usually ended up apologizing for. She was surprised because the day before he'd seemed a bit friendlier as they played the board games.

After several hours, many of the foods were prepared and placed in the refrigerator or covered and pushed to the back of the counter. Jaimyn could feel herself growing weary. She was glad when Gwen spoke up.

"Girls, that's enough for now. We all need to get outside and stretch our legs." She turned and looked out the window. "It's been snowing for the last hour, so I think we will be able to make some snow angels."

Shirley, who had joined them after she woke from her nap, began jumping up and down. "I want to make snow angels."

Gwen took off her apron. "I'll run up and get on something warmer. What about you, Jaimyn?"

"I'm okay. With a coat and boots, I'll be fine, but I do need to get them from our room."

"I'll get them." Gwen assured her and swished out of the kitchen.

Just then Ross reappeared. Shirley was running in circles.

"What's all the hullabaloo?" He asked.

"We're going out to make snow angels." Shirley

announced.

Ross looked up at his mother in surprise which turned into his usual frown. "Do you think that's a good idea? You could catch cold."

"Don't worry, I'm not going to lay down in the snow. I just want to get some fresh air."

Ross turned. "I'll get your coat and scarf."

Jaimyn watched him walk away. His perfectly shaped shoulders filled the doorway as he passed through.

"Ross worries too much. He is very sensitive and was pretty upset when I got sick. You see, he'd been working in another state for three years and hadn't been home for the holidays for a while. Right before I got sick, I made a big fuss about it and he told me there was nothing he could do about it. Then when I got sick and they called him, he came home immediately. He stayed with me day and night."

Jaimyn smiled. "That's nice."

"Unfortunately, he had to give up his job and I think he left a girl behind. He doesn't tell me much about it."

Jaimyn wondered if that's why he seemed so angry all the time. She could understand now why he wanted this holiday to be so perfect for his mother. No one wants to lose their mother and her coming close to death had really upset the man.

"What kind of work was he doing?"

"Oh, he's a lawyer. So, he can get a job anywhere. We are hoping he'll decide to stay closer to home this time."

"Do you all live in North Texas?" She asked, which made sense since they'd been on her flight.

"Yes, we live in Amarillo, he had been living in San Antonio."

"Wow, I live in Lubbock."

"We are almost neighbors. It's only a two-hour drive between our cities."

Jaimyn nodded. She wondered if there would ever be another chance of her seeing this family again once this holiday was over.

"So tonight, we have our thankful charade's game."

Jaimyn tilted her head. "Thankful charade game?"

"Yes, we all write down something we are thankful for and we act it out. The others have to guess what it is." Debra left the room to get her coat and scarf just as Gwen brought down Jaimyn's coat and boots. Jaimyn sat down and pulled on her boots.

Shirley came skipping down the stairs. "I'm ready to make snow angels."

"So am I." Jaimyn stood up and took the girl's hand. They walk out onto the back porch together.

Within minutes almost the entire family had joined them and each one was sprawled out on the ground lifting their arms and legs up and down making angels in the snow. Jaimyn laughed as hard as all the others, but her eyes were on Ross, who was not making angels. She just wanted to show him that she wasn't causing any problems being here.

When he caught her eye, he glared at her. When he didn't know she was watching, he had a small smile on his face, but she could see the concern in his eyes as he watched over his mother.

After five minutes, he reached down and pulled his mother to her feet. "That's long enough for you. Let's get you in and warmed up."

She reached out and patted his cheek. "Okay, Ross."

Jaimyn sat up and watched as he put his arm around the woman's should and led her to the house. It made Jaimyn's heart squeeze to see such dedication. Even if he did seem to be a grump, he definitely loved his mother.

Glen, their younger brother came over and held his hand out for Jaimyn. She took it and he pulled her to her feet.

"What's next on the plan?" She asked.

"We order pizza, sit around a big fire and…"

"Play Thankful Charades!"

His eyes opened wide. "You know."

"Debra told me; I just wasn't sure what we do before-hand. Pizza sounds good. Do you know of a place that will deliver?"

The teen shrugged. "Greg is in charge of it. I'm sure he's already found a place. Greg is very efficient."

"Well, that's a good thing, isn't it?"

The boy crossed his arms over his chest. "I guess, until it comes to trying to take charge of my life. He's always telling me what I should be doing in my future."

Jaimyn could see that it was an irritant to the youth. She patted his arm. "Greg, I had no parents and no brother and sister, but I would have loved to have had someone in my life who cared enough to help guide me. I'm sure your brother means well, but he just doesn't know how to go about doing it the right way. Why don't you try having a sit-down talk with him? Ask his ideas, and express yours. You may find that together, you'll come up with a plan that would be just right."

The boy blinked, as if the thought had never even been considered. His head moved up and down. "I'll do that. I mean, I know he does have some good ideas. Do you really think he'll listen to me?"

"If you act mature, I'm sure he will."

Glen stuck out his hand." Thanks Jaimyn. I'm glad you're here.

Jaimyn shook the boy's hand, enjoying the feel of her first brother sister conversation. She only hoped she was right and that Greg would respond to Glen the right way.

"I'll be praying for you, Glen." She stated, but knew she was going to have a short word with Greg as well.

When they stepped through the door, Ross was standing to the side of the fireplace. Debra was sitting beside it.

Glen pointed over his shoulder at Jaimyn with his thumb and stated, "She's pretty cool."

Ross didn't smile. Jaimyn slid her coat and boots off, then headed upstairs to brush her hair. She wanted to shake the man, but she had to keep in mind that she was an outsider here. Ross didn't have to like the fact that she was being treated like one of the family.

CHAPTER SIX

As promised, several large pizzas were delivered to the cottage. Greg had found a local pizza parlor in Sprucewood and offered a bit extra to have them brought to the farm. There was a plain pizza with cheese, a pepperoni pizza, one with veggies of all sorts, one with pineapple and smoked bacon. The restaurant also sent breadsticks, large bottles of soda and a bucket full of pasta.

Jaimyn was amazed at how much food was there. "I've never seen so much pizza in one place in my life, and I work in an office that orders in every Friday."

"Don't worry, it will all get eaten. You've never seen the Branson boys eat. And if there is any left over, it will disappear tomorrow, even after they all eat an entire Thanksgiving meal." Debra explained. "Ross will probably eat the most."

Everyone laughed, but Jaimyn noticed Ross didn't smile. He seemed nice enough but every time he looked at her, he began to frown. He was the only one not making her feel very welcomed in the group.

Gwen picked up a plate. "I'm first, everyone line-up and fill your plates."

Everyone fell in line and did as ordered. Jaimyn even ended up with three slices of pizza, two bread sticks and a small scoop of pasta. She took a seat beside Shirley and began eating.

"I love pizza!" Shirley shouted and took a big bite of her piece of pizza.

Jaimyn smiled at the child. "I love pizza too."

"Ross loves pizza the most." The child announced just as Ross entered the dining room and sat down. His plate was filled to the brim with about 6 slices.

Glen leaned over to Jaimyn. "That's just the beginning for Ross. The man can eat about twelve pieces."

Jaimyn was impressed. She did wonder how he kept in such good shape. For her, one piece of pizza meant twenty extra minutes of elliptical workout. She couldn't even imagine how much weight she was going to gain while celebrating Thanksgiving with this family.

She glanced down at the pizza and shrugged. *For this, it's worth a pound or two.*

Not long after, the whole family was gathered in the living room, the fire burning brightly. Everyone held a plate loaded with the yummy food. Gerald seemed to take over. He stood up.

"Now remember the rule. You all write down a full sentence about what you are grateful for this past year, then you act it out just like a regular game of charades." He scanned the faces. "No giving verbal clues either."

Jaimyn wasn't sure how this was going to go. She'd only played charades once when she was a child and had lived at one foster home. It was a good memory, so she hoped to make another pleasant memory in this game.

She picked up the piece of paper and a pencil and stared at the blankness.

What am I thankful for? She wondered, but not for long. After a few seconds she wrote on the page. *I am thankful for my new life as a Christian.*

Each family member stood up and acted out their phrase one at a time. Jaimyn found herself calling out single words and sentences along with the others. The laughter rang out around the room.

It took them all quite a while to figure out Jaimyn's and when they'd done it there was a reverential silence around the room for a few moments, until Amy said, "I think that's lovely, Jaimyn. Welcome to God's family."

Then it was Ross's turn.

He stood up and before he had even begun acting, Jaimyn knew his sentence was that he was thankful his mother was better. She just sat back and allowed the others to guess the answer. It gave her a chance to really look the man over.

Aside from his incredibly good looks and his grumpy attitude, there was a softness about him when it came to his family. When playing the game, he almost had a boyish look to him which she found rather endearing.

The entire family was kind, and from Amy's comment, she hoped that meant they were all Christians. Her relationship with Jesus was so new that she didn't feel very comfortable just blurting out the questions about their faith. Instead, she just sat by, laughing, joking and enjoying the evening.

It was nice to hear all the things that the family members were thankful for and she wished she could have a second turn because she would have liked to have added that she was thankful for this holiday with the Branson family.

~

After the game, everyone helped clear up the pizza and put the room in order. Most all of the food was prepared for cooking the next day, so the ladies all agreed to get up early and meet in the kitchen to make sure they got the timing for each item perfected.

The men agreed to sleep in and show up in time for the Macy's Thanksgiving parade, followed by the football game.

Finally, most of the family headed up to bed. Jaimyn was used to staying up later, so found herself a bit anxious about trying to settle in so early. "I'll sit here by the fire for a while if you don't mind." She whispered to Debra.

"That's fine. Ross usually closes up the house once we are all settled; that is when he is here."

"I'm glad for you that he was able to be here." Jaimyn found herself leaning over and giving the older woman a kiss on the cheek and wondering if her own mother's cheek had been as soft as this one.

Jaimyn searched the bookshelves and found a Bible. It was a different version than the New International Version she usually read, so she decided that might be interesting to peruse. She settled onto the sofa and began reading.

The noises above quieted and soon Jaimyn realized she was alone. She allowed her mind to rewind and review the entire day. It had been a bit exhausting but wonderful, from beginning to end. The girls had counted her as one of them. She'd gotten to help prepare a Thanksgiving meal and play charades. She'd made snow angels and not even once did she feel like an outsider.

Even Ross hadn't seemed as hard to get along with today. He'd laughed a few times and had spoken rather kindly to her once or twice. She wasn't sure why that mattered but it did. She wanted to fit into this family, so at least once she could say she'd had a family Thanksgiving.

Of course, she wasn't fooling herself completely. She knew this wasn't her own family and no amount of pretending would make it so. For now, she was just going to enjoy being accepted as one of them.

It was a bit sad to think that once this week was over, she might never see them all again.

As she sat, she heard footfalls on the steps. She turned. It was Ross.

Jaimyn straightened up.

"Sorry to disturb you. I just came down to check the locks." His voice was low and as usual he didn't smile.

"Yes, your mother told me you would. That's nice that they can all count on you to do that." The words tumbled out. She felt so awkward around the man.

His forehead line turned into a grim line. "Except the times I wasn't here so they couldn't count on me."

She knew he was referring to the fact that his mother had been so sick and he hadn't been on hand. But he had come home right away. She wished she could give him some comfort in that thought.

Ross moved around the house, checking doors and locks. Then stepped back into the living room. "Have you seen the stars?"

Jaimyn looked up at him. "Stars?"

"Yes, I know we have them in Texas, but honestly, you need to come outside and see them. Being up here in the mountains makes them seem so close."

She didn't have to be asked twice. She jumped right up. "Sure."

"Grab any coat and boots." He pointed at the front hallway.

Luckily hers were still in the hallway, so she slipped them on and in a moment met him at the back door. They both stepped out and stood on the porch. Ross had turned off the back light, so it was pretty dark out, however, the stars and moon lit the sky.

"Oh, it's beautiful." She took a deep breath of the cool air.

Ross stood still, staring at the sky. She wondered what he was thinking.

"You have no family?" he asked. A question which surprised her.

"Uhm, yes, I mean, no family. My mom died when I was a young teen and I never knew my father."

"I'm sorry and it was probably not my business. It's just that I've realized recently how important family is. I thought moving away, becoming a high-power lawyer would make me happy, but it didn't work that way at all. My family is all I have that makes me happy."

Jaimyn tried not to flash a look of pity. "Family is a wonderful thing, but it's not the thing that can make you truly happy."

Ross' smile disappeared. "A woman? Is that what you mean?"

She shook her head. "No, I'm thinking about Jesus. You see, I always thought if I had a family, I would be happy. But I discovered recently that having a relationship with Jesus fulfilled all that desire. I'd still like to have a family, but that would only be a plus."

Ross turned to face her. "I've gone to church my whole life; at least until I started law school. I wasn't happy. That was part of the reason I moved. I've been looking for something to fulfill me or satisfy me."

"But, did you have a relationship with Jesus?"

"No, not really. Some of the others in the family seem to. I guess I just didn't take the time to really figure the whole thing out. I couldn't see what that would have to do with anything."

"Well, I can only suggest you look into it. He can change everything." She smiled and looked away. "He made all the difference in my life."

Ross stared at her side profile.

"You're very lovely." His words were barely a whisper; Jaimyn wasn't sure if she'd even heard him correctly, but if she had, she couldn't help but be pleased. It had been a long, long time since a man had thought of her as lovely.

Just then Ross cleared his throat. "I'll think about what you've told me."

After a few more minutes, they both stepped back inside.

"Warm up by the fire again." Ross almost demanded. "I don't want anyone getting sick this holiday."

Jaimyn padded to the fire and stood by it, allowing the warmth to spread through her body. "MMM, this is nice. We don't get much snow in Texas and I have no fireplace. This is a real treat to me."

She turned to face Ross and was surprised to see he wasn't frowning at her. In fact, she was a bit surprised by the look on his face. He seemed almost mesmerized.

"The fire, highlights your hair. Makes is look like there are streaks of gold in it." His voice was very low. Suddenly, he shook his head and stepped back. “Hmph. I guess the house is locked up. I’m going to bed.”

Somehow, Jaimyn felt as if his words were also a command. “Yes, I’ll go up now too. Do we leave the fire burning?”

Ross nodded. “It’s not very big and will burn out soon.”

Jaimyn headed toward the stairs, then stopped and turned back to the man. “Ross, thanks for the stars.” She stated then traipsed up the stairs without waiting for an answer.

CHAPTER SEVEN

She pulled her Bible into her lap and opened it and spent the next half hour reading. Gwen and Shirley were still asleep, so she tried to stay quiet. When she finished reading, she tried to slip down the small ladder from the top bunk. When she reached the bottom, Shirley's eyes were wide open.

Jaimyn pressed a finger to her lips. "Shh."

Shirley nodded and rolled over, her thumb in her mouth and fell back asleep.

Jaimyn carried her clothes to the bathroom where she was able to take a quick morning shower. Without realizing it, she began singing, 'There is Power in the Blood.'

When she stepped out of the bathroom, Ross was leaning against the wall, as if waiting to go in. "Nice voice."

Jaimyn blushed. "You could hear me?"

He nodded.

"Oh, my. I was just feeling so happy. I always sing at home. I'm not used to having anyone around."

"You don't owe me an explanation. You can sing anywhere you want to. And I wasn't joking, you do have a nice voice." He turned and strolled away.

Jaimyn put her hands to her cheeks to feel if they were hot with embarrassment, shook her head and began to walk toward the stairs. It was nice the Ross had complimented her singing, but did it mean anything else?

As she stepped into the kitchen Debra looked up. "Good morning, Jaimyn."

"Debra, do you ever actually sleep?" Jaimyn laughed.

"Hmm, it's one of the side effects of motherhood. I think since the day that Ross was born, I've never slept more than six hours in a night. I suppose when I turn seventy, I'll start taking naps and catch up on all the sleep I've missed."

Jaimyn smiled. "I take naps now, whenever I can. Now, what do we do today?"

"Honestly, everything is already to go. It just needs to be stuck in the oven."

That was a surprise to Jaimyn, she always thought that Thanksgiving Day was the busiest; however, Debra was so organized they'd gotten it all prepared over the last two days.

Just then Ross came into the kitchen. "Mother, I was thinking of heading into Sprucewood. I say a flyer that said that one of the diners are serving breakfast tacos and coffee to go on Thanksgiving Day. I thought I'd grabbed enough for all of us."

Debra turned with a smile. "Ross, that's a wonderful idea. I know we usually all rely on chips and dip, but tacos sound wonderful." She turned to Jaimyn. "Have you seen the town yet?"

"Not close enough to stop anywhere."

Debra looked at Ross and nodded at Jaimyn.

Ross frowned.

Debra shook her head. "Why don't you go with Ross to get the tacos, see the town at the same time."

Jaimyn turned to look at Ross and noted his frown.

"I don't have to come along." Her heart dropped.

"I don't mind." Ross said.

Jaimyn wasn't sure he really meant it, but she wanted to go, so she nodded, walked to the door and grabbed her coat and boots. Ross held the front door open as she passed through it.

"We can take my car if you want." Jaimyn offered.

Ross nodded. "Better than this big suburban we rented for the whole family."

Ross followed her to the driver's side and held open the door for her. When she was in, he jogged around to the other side and got in. "You know how to drive this thing in the snow?" he asked.

"Well, I may have to go pretty slowly if the roads are icy."

She put the key in and turned on the ignition and steered the jeep down the driveway. They passed a few other cottages. There were a few people up and about but in general it was a quiet morning.

"This was a great idea!" Her voice was enthusiastic. "It will be interesting to see what breakfast tacos are like in Colorado."

"Nothing like Texas tacos, I'm sure." Ross added.

It didn't take long to reach the town. "Where are these tacos?"

Ross pointed down a street. "At the café called Dine in the Pines."

Jaimyn nodded and steered toward the café. Luckily, there weren't too many people out so early. She was able to find a parking spot right in front of the café. They both got out of the jeep and headed toward the doors.

"Don't you just get a kick out of the names of all the places in this town?" She asked. "I read them on line. Some gave me a good chuckle."

"Yeah, a bit too cute for me, but I'm sure it helps with tourism. My ex would have…" his voice dropped and he ended his sentence.

Jaimyn looked at him. "You, okay?"

"Yeah, I just don't like to talk about my ex."

"Oh, ok. I make a pretty good listener. You know, someone from outside the family."

Ross shook his head, then met her eyes.

"And, you know, you can always talk to Jesus about it."

Ross nodded. "I've been giving it some thought. And as far as my ex, there's nothing to say. We were dating and when I said I was moving back here, she said she was staying there. I don't think the split actually hurt either of us. We'd only been dating a while and it hadn't ever been a smooth type thing. I think, we were both trying to make something out of nothing. I know I was relieved when it was over."

Jaimyn just listened. She was glad that Ross was willing to open up to someone.

"I haven't shared that with anyone. I think the family believes I'm pining away for her. I guess I should have straightened that out in the beginning, but I've been upset about my mom and moving home and finding a new law office to work in has taken a lot of time."

"I think it would help if you did tell them. I'm sure they are concerned for your happiness and if you aren't unhappy about it, that's even better."

Ross nodded. “I’ll break the news to them tonight.” His lips formed a crooked smile. “Of course, then the match making will begin. They’ve been holding off because they all thought I had a broken heart.”

“Well, Shirley has already suggested I be your girlfriend.” Jaimyn laughed.

Ross’ eyes opened wide. “Really? Hmm, out of the mouth of babes.”

Jaimyn knew he was joking, but she was surprised he hadn’t put on a grim look again. She hadn’t meant to tell him about Shirley’s careless words. She wasn’t even sure why she’d done it.

They ordered what Jaimyn thought was enough tacos to feed a small army, but Ross assured her his brothers and father would eat the all. As they left the café, they were both laughing and joking around. It was obvious that whatever reserve Ross had, he’d lowered. Jaimyn enjoyed this version of Ross very much.

When they reached the kitchen at the Thanksgiving Cottage, with their load of taco’s, guacamole, salsa and chips, the others in the house were beginning to stir. Debra had slipped the turkey into the oven and the other items that needed to be cooked were lined up and marked with the times they needed to go into the over.

"I put some paper plates on the table for now. We can set out the nicer plates that the cottage has for our dinner."

Ross and Jaimyn headed toward the dining room.

"By the way, I took a walk the other day and found that they have some stables here. They offer sleigh rides. I signed the family up for about six tonight."

Jaimyn stared at him. Was she part of the family?

He must have read her mind.

"I counted you in too, is that okay?"

A silly grin formed. "Yes, that will be so much fun."

A swooshing sound came from behind her, and Jaimyn turned quickly to see what or who was behind her, but there was no one there. In the distance she thought she heard the door open and close.

She assumed one of the other adults had decided to go for a morning stroll, so she turned back around and began opening the bags and setting out the tacos in piles of bean and cheese, potato, egg and cheese, and bacon, egg and cheese. Her mouth watered from the aroma that drifted up from the hot tacos.

In several minutes, the entire family began to wander into the dining room, exclaiming over the tacos. Once they were all seated, Jaimyn looked around, Shirley wasn't at the table.

"Where is Shirley?" She asked.

Everyone looked around. "Isn't she still in bed?" Debra asked.

Gwen shook her head. "No, I just left the room."

Jaimyn turned to Ross. "Earlier, I heard the front door open. I think Shirley went outside."

Ross stood up abruptly. "Why didn't you say something then?" He glared at her.

"What I meant to say is that I heard the front door open and assumed someone went outside. I only now realize it was Shirley." She met his eyes evenly and lifted her chin.

His hands were clenched, but he apologized.

"You know Ross, we were talking about that sleigh ride. Maybe she heard us and wanted to go see the horses." Jaimyn suggested.

"She loves horses." Gwen added.

"Ok, are her coat and boots gone?" Ross asked as he headed toward the front door. Amy and Glen followed. They all put on their outdoor clothes. Jaimyn wished she could have gone too, but this was truly a family affair.

"Her boots and coat are here." Amy almost wailed.

Glen took his wife in his arms. "Don't worry. We'll find her. You stay here."

Amy shook her head. "No, I want to come too."

Debra moved close and put her arm around Amy. "I think the men can work faster without us. We'll start some warm soup and heat some blankets." She looked at Jaimyn. "Can you light a fire?"

Jaimyn nodded and headed toward the living room and began to put some logs into the fireplace. She also began praying for Shirley to be safe.

Debra pulled Amy and Gwen into the kitchen and made them work to keep everyone's mind off of things, but Jaimyn noticed Amy looking toward the door repeatedly.

Jaimyn moved closer to the woman. "I'm praying for Shirley." She whispered.

Amy's lips trembled a bit. "Thank you."

Jaimyn imagined that if things had been different, there would have been laughter and banter going on in the kitchen, but with Shirley's disappearance the ladies all worked quietly. She was sure in her heart that Shirley had gone to find the horses. The only question was, would she know the way or would she get lost?

About a half hour later, they all heard sounds from outside. Amy ran to the window. "It's Ross and he's carrying Shirley." She basically squealed with delight and ran toward the door.

Jaimyn slipped out to the living room, grabbed a small blanket that was over one of the chairs and took it into the kitchen. She put it in the microwave oven for a minute or two, then met them all in the hallway.

Amy was holding Shirley at this point, tears on her cheeks.

"Thank you, Ross."

Jaimyn moved closer. "I've got a warm blanket. Why don't we get her closer to the fire?"

Amy nodded and allowed Jaimyn to wrap the blanket around Shirley, who was shivering. Then Amy carried Shirley to the sofa near the fire.

After a few minutes, Shirley seemed to have warmed up some. She turned a bright smile to Jaimyn.

"I saw horses!"

Jaimyn sat on the sofa beside Amy. "Did you? That's nice, but next time you want to go see horses, you need to ask someone to go with you."

Shirley tilted her head and stared at Jaimyn, then she nodded. "I was cold."

Ross squatted down in front of Shirley. "If you want to go out again, ask me. I would have made sure you were dressed warmly."

Shirley glanced at her mother. "Are you mad, Mommy?"

"Yes, Shirley, a bit and scared too. I was worried that you were lost." She hugged the girl closer to her. "Promise Mommy you won't go out without someone with you ever again."

The girl's lip quivered. "I Pwomise Mommy."

Debra entered the room. "Let's all remember its Thanksgiving. The parade is on and there's plenty of chips and dip. Ladies, we can all finish making the meal."

Everyone sort of laughed, which broke through the seriousness of the moment and everyone got up and went about their regular morning activities.

Shirley was carried into the kitchen where she was fed a breakfast taco and then allowed to help make the mashed potatoes.

CHAPTER EIGHT

Jaimyn helped to set the table. The cottage was equipped with plates enough to serve twelve. They were beautiful with a pattern of fall leaves on them. A memory of dishes her mother had owned when she was a very young child flashed through her mind. She didn't often have these kinds of memories, but for just a moment the warmth of it rushed through her heart.

Ross came into the dining room and looked around. "This looks nice."

Jaimyn nodded. "It's nice that they have provided everything. It sure beats paper plates."

Ross smiled. "We always use my great grandmother's plates, but we didn't think we could bring those all with us. It's nice here, but seems strange."

"I'm sure having me here doesn't help. But for me, it's one of the best Thanksgivings ever."

Ross stepped closer and lifted her hand and gave it a squeeze. "I'm glad you're here. Everyone in the family likes you."

She laughed. "You weren't very happy to find me here."

"At first, but now ..." he stared into her eyes. "Now, I'm as happy as everyone in the family. You are special."

Jaimyn swallowed. She could feel warmth tingling in her hand and her heart beat a bit faster.

"Everyone come to the table!" Debra called out, which caused Jaimyn to jump and Ross dropped her hand and took a step back.

They both turned around and moved to their own spots at the table. Debra, Amy, Glen and Gwen carried platters full of food from the kitchen into the dining room. The last thing was the turkey which was set on the table in front of Gerald.

When they all sat, Gerald held out his hands and everyone at the table clasped hands. Gerald lowered his head and began to pray, thanking God for family and good food.

Jaimyn ate slowly, enjoying every bite and listening to the family banter and chatter. Shirley was full of stories about the howses she saw and Ross told them all he'd booked a sleigh ride for later in the evening, which excited everyone.

Ross, who had sat next to Jaimyn leaned over and whispered. "I'd like to have you sit with me."

She turned a surprised look on her face, but nodded slowly, a smile creeping across her face. When she looked up, everyone at the table was staring at her.

She felt a blush on her cheeks.

Shirley tilted her head. “Why’s everybody stwaring at Jaimyn?”

Amy leaned over and wiped the girl’s lips and tried to hush her, but she kept asking what was wrong with her Jaimyn’s face. “Her face is aww red.”

Finally, Ross cleared his throat. “Can this family please stop all this hullabaloo. Is there some reason I cannot ask a lovely woman to sit beside me on a sleigh ride?” His eyes met each family member’s eyes one at a time.

Each one lowered their eyes one at a time. Finally, Gerald broke the silence. “Well, let’s finish eating this excellent meal. Ladies, you’ve outdone yourselves this year.

Jaimyn lifted a fork full of mashed potatoes and stuck them in her mouth.

Gwen asked to have the stuffing passed to her and Debra sent the rolls around the table one more time.

Gerald suggested each person share their favorite Thanksgiving memory which was wonderful. Gerald and Debra both shared memories of their first Thanksgiving as a young married couple and not enough money to afford a turkey.

“What did you do, Gwandpa?” Shirley asked.

"We went to the Salvation Army and offered to help serve the homeless. That way we were doing something good and we both got a nice big plate of turkey and mashed potatoes."

As each one of them shared a memory, Jaimyn began to panic. She had no story to share. Every year of her life, she'd been in a different foster home, or orphanage. She'd been moved around so often, and even though each place tried to make things nice for the holidays, she never enjoyed them. Her heart had ached for a real family of her own to share the holidays with.

When it was her turn to speak, Jaimyn hesitated, then smiled. "I have to say that this is my favorite Thanksgiving so far. I have no wonderful memories of Thanksgivings in the past."

She noted the solemn faces around the table.

"Now, don't be sad. You all have given me the best day, full of great memories."

"I vote we invite Jaimyn to Thanksgiving every year, from now on." Glen's voice rang out.

Everyone nodded and lifted a hand in agreement.

This gesture truly blessed Jaimyn's heart.

Ross had raised his hand as well, which filled her with wonder.

~

After the meal, everyone pitched in to help with the washing up. Debra worked on covering dishes to save for the next day, while Jaimyn and Ross worked on the dishes. She had her hands in the sink, bubbles everywhere, washing dishes and handing them to Ross, who would place them into the washing machine.

"I've never understood why we wash dishes, to put them in the dishwasher." His voice was full of mirth.

"Oh, it's just to get the worst off. I consider my washing machine as a sanitizer. When you consider it that way, it makes all the difference."

"You make me see so many things in a different way." He stepped closer to her and bent over, placing a small kiss on her forehead.

~

It had started to snow again, and Jaimyn was excited about the evening's sleigh ride.

Whenever she remembered Ross asking to sit with her, she'd start to feel the same tingling through her body. She was excited, but at the same time a bit upset that she was feeling these things. She knew when this holiday was over, she would go home and Ross would go home and that would be the end of it. There was no point in thinking anything could grow between them; even that kiss had been sweet, but nothing to expect a future relationship on.

Besides, a kiss on the forehead could be his way of telling her she was like a little sister to him. She had to keep in mind that once they all left the Holiday Cottages, Lubbock and Amarillo were two hours apart. She wasn't interested in a long-distance relationship and two hours was just on the verge of too long. Perhaps an hour apart could be made to work.

Just then Glen walked by. "I'm so full." He patted his stomach.

"So am I."

"Oh, and just to let you know. I had a talk with my dad and he really listened to me."

"I'm so glad. I've been praying about it."

The boy tucked his head slightly. "I have been too."

Jaimyn's eyes lit up. "Are you a believer?"

"Yes, but I haven't been paying much attention to my relationship with God. You saying you would pray for me, jolted something inside of me and reminded me that I could be praying too."

Jaimyn reached out and touched his hand. "That's very good to know."

"I'll always remember this Thanksgiving, thanks to you." Glen smiled. "I hope Uncle Ross and you start dating."

Jaimyn sucked in a breath. “Glen! Ross and I are only friends who barely know each other. I live two hours away from him, so I don’t foresee us starting to date.”

Glen shook his head. “it’s not that far. We actually live in a place called Tulia which is only one hour from you.”

Jaimyn was surprised. That could mean something different if Ross were actually interested in her.

Glen walked away, leaving Jaimyn to her own thoughts.

~

At the appointed time, the entire family gathered in coats, scarves and boots. Ross said that the sleigh would come to the cottage to pick them all up.

Shirley was jumping up and down. “We’s gonna see my howses again.”

Her mother, Amy, grabbed her hand. “Shirley, you stay right beside me all the time. I don’t want to lose you again.”

Shirley cocked her head. “You didn’t lose me. I went to see the howses.”

“Okay, well we are going to be riding in a sleigh pulled by horses, so stay with me.”

Shirley plopped her thumb in her mouth and took her mother's hand with her other hand. They joined the others at the front door.

Ross watched out the front door. "Here comes the sleigh." He turned back and met Jaimyn's eyes. She smiled.

The family all pressed out the door, chattering and excited. Ross and Gerald assisted everyone into their seats, then they both climbed in too. Ross, sat beside Jaimyn. The man who drove the sleigh was named Dixon. He had an infectious smile and laugh which put them all at ease'

As they rode throughout the fields between the cottages. Dixon led them all in song; singing 'Over the River and Through the Woods' and even a few early Christmas songs. Their cheeks were all rosy red from the cold air.

The sun was beginning to set, but the moon was bright enough to light up the sky. Ross reached over and took Jaimyn's hand in his. "Are you enjoying yourself?"

"Mmm, it's wonderful. The moon is so big, I feel as if I could just reach out and touch it. There's never anything like this at home." She thought for a moment. "Well, in all honesty, I don't get outside much at home. I work all day and … I don't go out much as night."

"No dates?" Ross asked.

"Not often."

"So, basically the playing field is clear?"

She stared at him. "What does that mean?"

Ross smiled and moved closer to her. "That means, there's no one else I have to compete against to get close to you?"

Jaimyn gulped. "No, that is…" She gave a questioning look. "We live pretty far apart. I didn't think you'd want to… you know, play the field."

"Glen informed me earlier; we only live an hour apart."

"Yes, but are you actually interested in… me?"

Ross tossed his head back and laughed, a deep, hearty laugh. "Yes, Jaimyn. I am very interested in you. I know I started seemingly irritated that you were here, but you've changed my mind and my heart. By reminding me of my relationship with Jesus, I was able to forgive my last girlfriend and that somehow opened my heart to a new beginning. One which I hope to start off with you."

Jaimyn's mouth dropped open. She wasn't sure what to say. It was all so wonderful, so new, so seemingly impossible, and yet something she too desired.

.

CHAPTER NINE

They all hated for the sleigh ride to end because it signaled the end of the day and not one of them wanted this Thanksgiving to end. As they stepped out of the sleigh, Debra noted the mood.

"Remember, we still have pumpkin pie and the wishbone."

A few smiles reappeared.

"Jaimyn and me gets to do the wishbone this year, wight?"

Ross picked her up and tossed her up and down a few times. "That's right, little one."

Happily, they all trudged up to the Cottage.

"Glen, build up the fire, Gwen get out the pie plates…" Debra called out as they all began to strip off their coats and boots. The family gathered in the living room, where the fire quickly began to warm them all.

Before long, everyone had a slice of pumpkin or pecan pie and the family chatter went on. Everyone tried their best to include Jaimyn but when memories were brought up, she wasn't able to participate. However, she was able to close her eyes and imagine the things as they must have looked when they happened.

"I wish I could see a photo album of you all when you were younger. That would help me be able to picture these things so much better."

"Next yeaw, you can come to Grandma's house and see the pictures." Shirley threw out innocently. "Riwt Grandma?"

Debra looked at Ross. His smile hadn't disappeared. "Yes, that's a great idea. Actually, what about Christmas this year?"

Jaimyn lifted her head, her mouth dropped open in surprise, but her eyes sought Ross'. He nodded.

"I'd like that. Of course, we can revisit the idea when it gets closer to the date, in case anything changes." Jaimyn added, thinking that by then Ross may have met someone closer to home.

"It's time for the wishbone." Debra announced.

Shirley jumped up and down. "You and me, Jaimyn. We get to make wishes."

Jaimyn wasn't sure what making a wish on a wishbone meant, but she was game for anything.

Debra came out of the kitchen holding the turkey wishbone which she'd cleaned and bleached and handed it to Shirley.

"Now, tell Jaimyn what she has to do." Debra suggested to Shirley. The girl nodded.

"Jaimyn, what we do is, we each grab the wishbone. We make a wish and pull until the wishbone breaks."

The look on Jaimyn's face was one of confusion.

Amy spoke up. "The person who ends up with the biggest half gets their wish."

Shirley's head moved up and down. "You weady?"

Jaimyn smiled. "Yes, have you made a wish?"

Shirley nodded. "You make one too. Close your eyes and pull."

At the same time, they both closed their eyes and pulled. Jaimyn didn't pull very hard, since she knew she was new at it and Shirley was on the other side. However, it was actually hard to break the wishbone in half. Finally, it split.

Both opened their eyes. Shirley had the bigger half, which made Jaimyn sigh with relief.

"I win. I get my wish."

Jaimyn reached over and gave the girl a hug. "That's right. I'm so happy for you."

Shirley looked up. "Didn't you want your wish?"

"Yes, but I'm glad you won. Maybe next year, I'll win."

Shirley nodded. "Do you want to know what my wish was?"

Jaimyn smiled. "Only is you want to tell me."

"I wished Uncle Ross would marry you, so you could spend all Thanksgivings with us."

Jaimyn gulped. Something similar had been her wish as well.

~

As the night wore on, each family member eventually drifted off to their rooms, once again leaving Jaimyn and Ross alone in the living room. Gerald had been the last to leave and had turned around with a wink. "Good night you two."

Jaimyn felt strange, purposely staying behind, hoping to spend more time with Ross, but she did want to.

As Gerald walked out of the room, Ross turned to Jaimyn. "Well, I never thought they'd all go to bed."

His words seemed to lighten the mood.

"Believe me, they all know what they were doing."

"Does that mean they didn't want us to be alone together?" Jaimyn bit her bottom lip. She thought they all liked her.

"No, they know I wanted to be alone with you, and they thought it would be funny to make me wait."

"And did you?"

"Did I what?"

"Want to be alone with me?"

Ross scooted closer on the sofa to her. "Indeed, I did. In fact, I do." He put his hand under her chin and tilted her face up; leaned forward and pressed his lips to hers.

The two sat for a long time, talking, sharing things about their childhoods, past relationships, hurts, hopes, dreams, fears. By the end of the evening, they knew much about one another and still wanted to know more.

“I can’t believe this whole thing is over tomorrow.” Jaimyn’s voice lowered sadly.

Ross gave a quizzical look. “Over?”

“Yes, I was only signed up to stay here until tomorrow.”

“Us too, but that doesn’t mean this whole thing is over. I think of this holiday as only the beginning of something very special. A relationship with a lovely, good, Godly woman. Pretty much what I’ve looked for my whole life.”

His words touched her soul, she leaned her head back and snuggled into his arm which he encircled her with thinking that he was what she had been looking for her whole life as well.

~

The following week at work, Jaimyn was refreshed and happy. She too was able to show photos of her lovely vacation and tell the fun story of having to share a cottage with the Branson family. Her best friend frowned.

"You could have come on the cruise with me. At least you know my family."

Jaimyn smiled. "That would have been nice, but honestly, I was really wanting to see snow and mountains. I expected to have a peaceful time away by myself, but it all ended up to be nice with the family. They welcomed me in."

Kathy grabbed Jaimyn's phone and scrolled through the photos again. "Who is this?" She turned to phone around. It was a photo of Ross.

"That's Ross."

"Ross? He looks a bit grumpy."

"Yes, he wasn't too happy I was there…at least in the beginning." Her voice drifted.

Kathy glared at her. "Sounds like a story…go on, I'm waiting."

Jaimyn giggled. "Well, he wasn't happy I was there, but his family liked me, and his niece wanted me and him to… be boyfriend and girlfriend. So, we ended up spending a lot of time together."

Kathy sat down; her mouth opened wide. "Really, and are you ever going to see him again?"

Jaimyn's smile dropped. "Well, he only lives about an hour or so from here, however, there wasn't any promise made. There were some innuendos, but I can't expect a man to want to travel that far for a relationship. I mean, I'd be willing to travel to see him, off and on, and we could meet in the middle."

Kathy whistled. "Wowsers… you must really like him. What about, you know your new relationship with Jesus?"

"Well, his family are Christians, but he's not been close to God in a few years. I think some of our conversations have stirred the desire in him to serve Jesus. But at this point, its not really anything for me to worry about. As I said, I doubt he'll want to have a long-distance relationship."

Kathy gave her a quirky smile. "Well, I guess we'll see. The man would be a fool to let a little thing like an hour's drive keep him from some one as special as you." She gave Jaimyn a hug and then turned back to her own desk.

Jaimyn began typing. It was good to be back at work, and able to keep her mind off her telephone. She had found herself looking at it, checking it several times, hoping Ross would call. She was feeling a bit disappointed, but knew she needed to get herself in hand.

At least I'm no worse off than I was before the holiday, and I've got some great memories.

She tried to tuck away the thoughts and her hopes of a relationship with Ross.

One thing was clear though, she no longer wanted to spend the holidays alone. In the future she would join other families, or even better, open her own home to others at her church who were by themselves for the holiday.

"Excuse me, Jaimyn."

She looked up. It was one of the men from the office named Darrell.

"Yes."

"Several of us are going out for wings after work today. I wondered if you would like to join us?"

Jaimyn was surprised. She'd never been asked before and if she had been would probably have said no. She squinted at the man slightly. He was jovial, although young.

"A group?" she asked.

"Yes, there are four other ladies and a few of us gents."

"Then, I think that would be nice. What's the name of the place, I can meet you all there."

"Buffalo Wild Wings. It's just two miles, straight down the main street from here."

"Yes, I know it. So, six thirty then?"

The man nodded. "See you there."

Jaimyn watched him walk away. She wondered if she'd just agreed to a gathering of workers, or a date.

~

Later that evening, Jaimyn lounged at home. The gathering of workers at Buffalo Wild Wings had been fun. It had definitely not been a date, as Darrell had also invited a girl from the office named Nancy, who he was very fond of.

Jaimyn didn't regret going, but she'd probably never do so again. They were a young crowd, giddy and silly. She was just too serious for them. She also felt that some of their jokes and conversation did not line up with her new relationship with Jesus.

Now, as she sat alone, she wondered just where she did fit in and now that Thanksgiving was over, the next holiday was soon to be upon her. Christmas. Once again feelings of loneliness filled her. She'd really hoped that Ross would have called. But there was no use crying over spilt milk.

Just then her phone rang. Jaimyn pulled it out of her pocket and swiped. She didn't recognize the number.

"Hello."

"Hello, is that you, Jaimyn? It's Ross."

Jaimyn swallowed.

"I'm sorry I haven't called before this. The whole family ended up with terrible colds after the trip and even I've been in bed for a week. I hope you didn't think I'd forgotten you."

"No, not at all. Well, at least…."

Ross laughed. “I was worried that’s what you thought. But, darling. I’m just as crazy about you as I was in Colorado. In fact, I may be even crazier now than then. I know I’ve been going stir crazy through this illness.”

“I hope you and the family are all better.” Jaimyn stated. Her heart was beating happily at his voice.

“Yes, we are. Now… when can I come see you.”

.

CHAPTER TEN

A YEAR LATER

"Jaimyn, you get to break the wishbone again this year." Shirley danced into the bedroom in her lovely flower girl dress.

"Really, but I got to do it last year." Jaimyn turned around once more in front of the full-length mirror to see the complete full effect of her wedding gown.

"But you didn't win. So, you get to have one more chance and this year its Uncle Ross' turn."

Jaimyn patted the child's head. "Alright, you imp. Now, go join your mother so we can have this wedding."

Shirley skipped out of the room, her small basket of rose petals precariously swirling on her arm. Jaimyn wondered if there would be any petals left by time the girl had to walk down the aisle.

Just then, Debra stepped into the room. "Here is your veil. I used the steamer to get the wrinkles out." She held out a breathtaking veil made of the finest lace.

Jaimyn took it and placed it on her head. "Debra, it's lovely." She spun around. "Are you sure you want me to use your mother's veil?"

"Yes. I wore it for my wedding. Amy wore it when she married Greg, Gwen will wear it one day when she marries, and you, my precious new daughter, are more than welcome to wear it." She moved across the room and gave Jaimyn a hug.

This was the closest Jaimyn had ever come to having a real mother's hug since she was a young child. It brought tears to her eyes.

"I'll be proud to wear it. I hope we didn't ruin the family's holidays by deciding to get married on Thanksgiving. We felt that since we'd met on Thanksgiving, it would be the best day to get married."

"Of course not. We all think it's wonderful. It will be a great memory for all of our future Thanksgiving get togethers. I'm so glad you and Ross were able to work things out long distance all these months."

"Yes, but I'll be glad to walk away from my job and move into our home here, closer to all of you." Jaimyn spoke truthfully. Recently, she'd realized that her job was not something that made her happy, and she looked forward to finding a new one, although Ross assured her, he could afford for her to stay home and be a lady of leisure if she chose.

The ladies hugged again. A knock on the door drew their attention. Debra opened the door. Gerald was standing there with his eyes closed.

"Is everyone decent?" He called in.

Debra walked over and kissed his cheek. "You may open your eyes dear. Jaimyn is all ready to go."

He opened his eyes. "It's time, Jaimyn." He smiled at her. "You look very beautiful. In fact, I think I've only seen one bride ever as lovely." His eyes met Debra's and she blushed.

Jaimyn wondered if she and Ross would still feel that way in thirty years. She could only hope and pray that their relationship together and with God would grow more lovely as the years went by.

That was the greatest thing, knowing that Ross had truly come to know and love Jesus.

She moved across the room and took Gerald's arm. The man had agreed to walk her down the aisle since she had no earthly father to give her away and since he was soon to be her father-in-law, he'd offered.

Debra hurried ahead of them so she could sit in the front row of the church. Jaimyn and Gerald moved out into the hallway. The music began and Shirley led the way perfectly dropping petals every few steps. She was followed by Kathy and Gwen who were the bride's maids. Finally, with one last glance at Jaimyn, Gerald began to walk the aisle with her holding onto his arm and saying a silent prayer of thanksgiving as she moved.

Jaimyn was nervous, but Gerald's arm gave her strength and when she looked up and met Ross's eyes, a calmness flowed through her. Marrying Ross was the right thing to do, it was the gift God had given her.

When she stepped up beside Ross, they took hands then turned to face the pastor, ready to speak their vows and begin their life together.

~

Later that evening, as they danced the last dance together, Jaimyn leaned into Ross's arms.

"You know, this morning, Shirley told me that I get to break the wishbone again this year because I didn't win last year."

Ross smiled.

"But she was wrong, you know. I did win."

Ross gave a quizzical look.

"I made a very special wish and it came true, so I consider that a win."

"Oh, really Mrs. Branson." He leaned closer and kissed her cheek. "What was that wish?"

"I wished that you and I would have a future together, and it came true."

Ross tilted her head up and pressed his lips to hers. "I'm so glad you made that wish. But, for me, I wasn't wishing, I was praying.

~

Two hours later, after all the good byes were said, and hugs given by every family member to the new sister, they flew off together to Denver. From the airport, they drove slowly, enjoying all the scenery, until they reached the Thanksgiving Cottage where they planned to spend their honeymoon.

Much later, standing outside together, looking at the bright stars, Jaimyn cuddled closer in Ross' arms.

"All I have to say is I'm thankful that we both booked this cottage at the same time last year. That will forever be my favorite Thanksgiving, ever."

He held her close and whispered, "No my dear, that was only the beginning of a lifetime of perfect Thanksgivings for us."

She nodded and their lips met.

TERESA IVES LILLY'S ninth grade teacher inspired her writing by allowing her to take a twelfth-grade creative writing course during the summer. After that, it has been her passion and dream to write. However, until her Salvation in 1986 when she discovered the genre of Christian Romance, Teresa did not even try. Since then, she has gone on to write numerous novellas and novels including several published by the Christian publisher *Barbour Books*. Teresa lives in San Antonio, Texas where she and her husband are close to their three grown children and grandchildren. Teresa believes God let her be born "at such a time as this" to be able to write and share her stories which she hopes will encourage you, the reader, to seek God and Salvation.

Made in the USA
Monee, IL
15 July 2023